Picnic with Oliver

by Mika Song

HARPER

An Imprint of HarperCollinsPublishers

www.harpercollinschildrens.com

ISBN 978-0-06-242950-6

The artist used ink and watercolor to create the illustrations for this book.

Typography by Mika Song and Chelsea C. Donaldson

18 19 20 21 22 SCP 10 9 8 7 6 5 4 3 2 1
❖
First Edition

Oliver and Philbert are best friends. They do everything together.

I have an idea.

The two friends find a perfect spot by the pond.

Oliver unpacks all their things,
but Philbert can't wait.

While Philbert sets sail, Oliver makes lunch.

In the distance, storm clouds creep in,

and it begins to rain on poor Philbert.

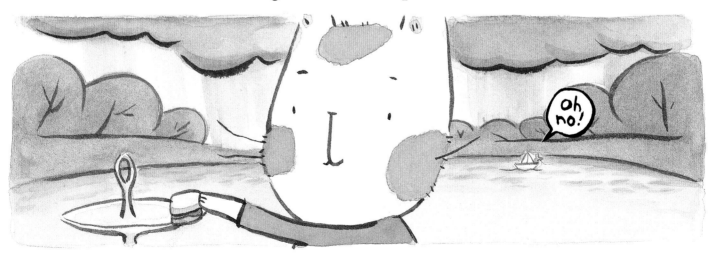

Suddenly the pond is a rough sea. Philbert's boat is much too small for the big waves.

Oliver thinks quick.

Oliver and Philbert return home and are quite pleased.
They have everything they need for their picnic.